Finding Baba Yaga

Selected Other Works by Jane Yolen

Briar Rose

B.U.G. (Big Ugly Guy) (with Adam Stemple)

Curse of the Thirteenth Fey

The Devil's Arithmetic

Except the Queen (with Midori Snyder)

Mapping the Bones

The One-Armed Queen

A Plague of Unicorns

Sister Light, Sister Dark

Snow in Summer

Sword of the Rightful King

White Jenna

JANE YOLEN

Finding Baba Yaga

A SHORT NOVEL IN VERSE

A TOM DOHERTY ASSOCIATES BOOK

NEW YORK

FINDING BABA YAGA

Copyright © 2018 by Jane Yolen

"Baba Yaga Has Tea with Kostchai the Deathless" was originally published in *Liminality* magazine in 2015; "Mortar/Pestle" was originally published in *Mythic Delirium,* issue 1.4, in May 2015; "Feisty Girls" was originally published in *Mythic Delirium,* issue 3.3, in February 2017

Cover photography by Shutterstock.com
Cover design by Jamie Stafford-Hill
Interior illustration by Kathleen Jennings

A Tor.com Book
Published by Tom Doherty Associates
175 Fifth Avenue, New York, NY 10010
www.tor.com

Tor* is a registered trademark of Macmillan Publishing Group, LLC.

ISBN 978-1-250-16387-5 (ebook)
ISBN 978-1-250-16386-8 (trade paperback)

First Edition: October 2018

*For the Baba Yaga women in my life—Heidi Stemple,
Elizabeth Harding, Malerie Yolen Cohen, Mira
Bartok, Betsy Pucci Stemple, Joanne Lee Stemple—
and in memory of the greatest Baba Yaga of all,
Marilyn Marlow. Tough love personified.*

Table of Contents

Foreword

Here's what you need to know about Baba Yaga, the great, iconic, Russian fairy tale witch. She lives in a house in the wood that walks about on chicken feet. She calls to it: "Turn about, little house, turn to me," and it rotates until its front door is right before her. She flies around in the sky in a human-sized mortar (the kind used for grinding herbs), which she steers with a pestle. She has an iron nose and iron teeth. Smart and bold little girls like Vasilisa work for her and are rewarded, but Baba Yaga devours naughty boys. Some stories say she has a fence around her house made of the bones of the children she has eaten. But that fence also migrated in storyland to the house of the Hansel and Gretel witch, so I have put it there instead.

Baba Yaga represents the ageless life force. She's a magical crone, once both feared and worshipped by Russian peasants. In fact, these days around the world, she is better known than any other Russian folk tale character, more popular than Vasilisa, Kostchai the Deathless, or Firebird. She's appeared in novels, graphic novels, movies, and TV series. Added to that, Baba Yaga is both my hero and the nightmare figure in my dreams. I have taken all the characters, added a modern family, and the rest is a novel in verse that mixes Russia folklore and American realism.

—Jane Yolen

PS: In July 2013, I discovered the very strange website *Once*

Upon a Blog . . . Fairy Tale News (http://fairytalenewsblog
.blogspot.co.uk), which featured an ongoing set of weekly
posts voiced by Baba Yaga as a Lonely Hearts columnist.
Originally posted on *The Hairpin,* "Ask Baba Yaga" has since
been collected and published as *Ask Baba Yaga: Otherworldly
Advice for Everyday Troubles* by Taisia Kitaiskaia (Andrew
McMeel, 2017). *Ask Baba Yaga* is hilarious and provocative,
and these poems would not exist without her posts.

Finding Baba Yaga

You Think You Know This Story

You think you know this story.
You do not.
You think it's about a princess who runs
from a wicked king.
It is not.

You think it is about a charming prince
who rescues, relieves, releases
a maiden from her tower.
It is not.

Surely there must be pumpkin, huntsman,
coach, some dwarves, a troll,
riding hood, ring, wand.
There is not.

Stories retold are stories remade.
A sorrowing girl in a house.
An old witch with iron fillings.
A hut in the wood,
in the meadow, in the hood.

This is a tale
both old and new,

borrowed, narrowed,
broadened, deepened.

You think you know this story.
You do not.

CHAPTER ONE

The
Last Fight

Papa Says, Mama Says

It is not a conversation,
but serial monologues,
each one waiting
for that breath space
to say his own,
her own
piece.

Peace.
There is no peace
in this house,
only strips of paper,
tatters of cloth,
slivers of glass,
slit lips and tongues.
I pick up the shards
and put me to bed
every night.

Wake up in pieces
every day
because of what
Mama says,
Papa says.

I don't say.

Argument

At first no one screams,
trading whispered accusations.
Papa means, Mama means.

At first no one listens,
words like *filth* hang between us,
tears glisten.

At first no one forgets,
anger anchored way too deep
in an ocean of regrets.

At first no one thinks it matters,
Papa said. Mama said.
Night shatters.

At first no one denies
the sliver of surprise
beneath each glossy nail.

At first.

The Word That Shatters Trust

Papa does not let us swear.
Words, he says, bind the world,
otherwise we shatter the trust
God gave us in this life.

Good words, *logos* he calls it,
God's words in the beginning.
It's why he's so careful with them,
doling them out like a miser
on Christmas morning.

But bad words, he calls *bogus*,
confusing anger with sin.
Sometimes a bad word
is punctuation to a bad day,
makes us laugh, gives us courage,
lifts the heart.

Swearing can be held too tight in the heart,
Speaking it aloud, an artifact, an art.

The Goodest Word, The God-est Word

Has Papa ever said *love* without warning?
Has he ever said *love* with warming?
Has he ever said *love* without worry?
Has he only said *love* in a weary way?

Has he ever spoken,
Has he ever really said the word?
Love.

Soap in the Mouth

I simply say the bathroom word,
the one written on school walls.
The common one in the mouths
of angry teachers when chalk breaks.

And Papa calls me filth,
takes the Dove soap,
jams it in my mouth
before I can apologize, turn away.

There's no anger in what he does,
only deadly purpose.
He says words have power.
The power to make you feel dirty
even while getting clean.

Angels are always clean.
Through the bubbles I ask:
What about feather mites?
This time I remember to duck.

The Taste That Lingers

Soap on the tongue lingers.
You cannot spit it out,
cannot swallow it down.

It is as if that word still
tingles in my mouth, a reminder
of my father's distaste.

I think of Nathaniel
in my kindergarten class,
the only Jew I've ever known.

He told us how he learned
to read Hebrew prayers
by licking each letter.

They were strange and difficult,
smeared with honey
on the rabbi's book.

Words shouldn't be dirty or clean
but definitely sweet,
on the tongue, in the mind.

Nathaniel taught me that
before I knew the alphabet.
Papa would have been horrified:

at the letters,
at the honey,
at the Jew.

Behind A Closed Door

No words can unlock the door,
can find the key to my cage.
I swing my head like an old elephant
well used to captivity. I pace the floor,
count the steps between bedroom walls.

In mourning, I wait for morning.
Waiting is a coffin that confines me,
defines me.

I have to find the courage.
I have to find
the key.

Fence of Bones

Mama unlocks the door after Papa leaves,
the accusations between us
like a fence made of bones.

Long leg bones the railings,
arm bones the gate,
eye socket the lock,
middle finger bone the key.

We sit at the table,
coffee growing cold.
My mother grows old,
her face skull-like.
I watch her fast-forward
into a bleaker future.

Standing, I fling the coffee cup,
call her *witch*,
wish I could believe
in the magic of escape.

I will be well punished for that word
    as well.

The Porch Tells Me to Go

I sit in the porch rocker
where once I was a child.
The porch tells me to go.
The steps tell me to get away.
The driveway tells me to flee.
The old tree tells me to leave.
The swing hung on a limb,
where once I could almost touch the sky,
Papa's hands on my back, pushing,
before he was pushed into preaching,
that swing says nothing.

A car rushes down the street,
as I should,
singing a tireless song.

The rocker tells me to stay,
its voice a comfort.

But the road beckons,
the highway calls,
the day seduces.

Another word I'm not allowed to speak
Unless it's to condemn.

If I'd Made a Plan

If I'd made a plan
it wouldn't be this one.
If I'd packed a bag,
it wouldn't be my backpack.
If I'd left a letter,
I couldn't have written a word.

See, it all begins and ends
with that.
A word.
But which word:
love,
regret,
goodbye?

CHAPTER TWO

The Runaway

Never Look Back

Never look back at the porch,
the house, the bedroom,
the secrets.

Look ahead.

Never look back at the kitchen,
the soap, the lock, the key,
the silence.

Look ahead.

Whatever I'm wearing, I wear.
Whatever's in my pockets, I have.
Whatever I think I know, I know.
Whatever I forget is gone.

Goodbyes are not an option.
Only so-longs.

All Paths Lead Here

I run out of the house,
across the road,
forget to look both ways,
hear the door slam behind me.

No one follows to beg me to come home.
No one sends me a letter.
No one tracks my email.
No one calls 9-1-1.

All paths lead here,
the Baba tells me later.
No paths lead out.

The Hardest Part

The hardest part is not looking back.
The hardest part is looking ahead.
The hardest part is not turning the corner.
The hardest part is crossing the street.
The hardest part is not passing the school.
The hardest part is walking out of town.
The hardest part is not thumbing a ride.
The hardest part is getting in the car.
The hardest part is not getting out of the car.
The hardest part is going in the 7-Eleven.
The hardest part is not stealing the chocolate bar.
The hardest part is walking out the door.
The hardest part is not eating the chocolate.
The hardest part is . . .

There is no easy part.

Phoning a Friend

With almost the last charge
of my cell phone battery
I phone a friend.

She says come over,
have dinner,
stay the night.
I who have never
come over, had dinner,
stayed the night
before.

When I get there,
my mother's battered car
idles in their driveway.
I don't go in.
Only then do I remember—
I have no friends.

What Happens Next

There's only
forward,
outward,
onward.

There's only
inward,
downward
afterward.

There's only away.

A Long Walk to Nowhere

Your back wears out before your feet do.
Your shins complain before your stomach.
It's no longer easy to live on candy bars
stolen from the corner store, though the map's good.

Rain takes a long time to dry on your clothes.
Sleeping on the ground is harder than you think.
Learning to pee in the woods, in the scrub,
means unlearning years of potty training.

Hunger is a bad companion and a worse friend.
Somewhere becomes a nightmare.
I knock on no doors, make no phone calls.
Nowhere becomes my destination.

You can find it on the blank spaces
of any free map in any old store.
Just turn a corner of your mind,
and it's there.

Sleeping Rough

First night I lie on a picnic table
looking up at the stars.
All I can pick out are Orion and the Dipper.

Maybe I can borrow a library book.
Learn the names of galaxies, constellations.
Find out about the moon and tides.

Remember then I have no library card with me.
I have no library to go to.
I turn angrily, fall off the table.

See stars.

Washing Away the Filth

It's too cold to wash in the river.
Besides, I've left all that soap behind.
I think of it suddenly, the Dove resting
in its plastic nest, wondering
when Noah will send it forth.

My mind wanders over the endless sea
of my leaving. There is an ocean
between me and the safety of some Ararat.
Who knows what toothy creatures
hunt in the dark waves.

I'm filthy now just as Papa always said
There's no sea, no ocean, no rainfall,
that can ever wash these stains away.

Stain—almost an anagram for Satan,
one small letter difference.
Things always come back
to the word.

This Is Not a Fairy Tale

Expect no princes.
Expect no magic rings.
Expect no glass slippers.
Expect no fairy godmothers.
Expect no singing dwarfs.
Expect no talking dragons.

Expect only
seven deadlies delivered:
exhaustion,
boredom,
regret,
hunger,
anger,
danger,
death.

All part of God's taketh away.

The Last Road

I turn off the highway onto an A road,
cross to a B road, sidestep onto a thin blue line,
numberless but still paved.

Cars brush by me, one so close, my map
flies into the air on its own wings,
a fat, lazy pigeon, not a dove.

When I find the map again,
along the shoulder of the road,
the page I'm on is crossed with tire tracks.

Finding a space in a hedgerow, I plow on through.
My options narrow to this: A simple path
into a wood of ghostly white trees.

Above me a murder of crows discuss dinner.
A wind puzzles through the birches.
Like the hero in any good tale, I boldly walk in.

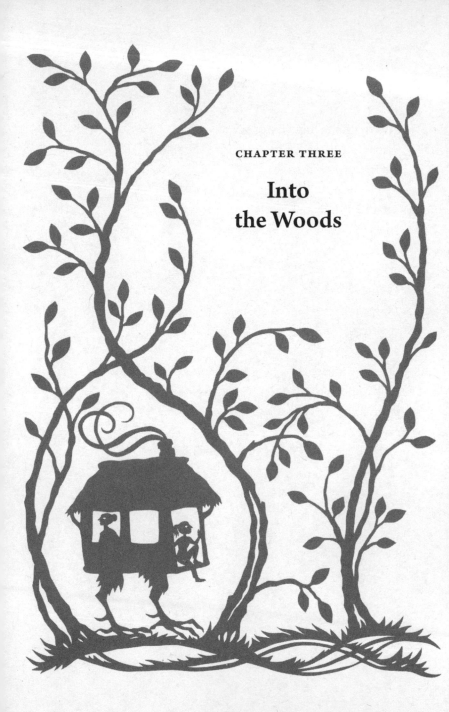

CHAPTER THREE

Into
the Woods

Counting Stones

This is the abacus of my journey.

A stone for the days I was on the road: 7.
A stone for the nights I slept rough: 6.
A stone for the days I saw no one to talk to: 5.
A stone for the days I had nothing to eat: 4.
A stone for the days I longed to go home: 3.
A stone for the days I tried to return: 2.
A stone for the doors I walked out of: 1.

A heavy heart with all those stones
weighing me down.
A February of them.

I leave the abacus in the woods.

The Forest Opens Like a Yawn

The forest opens like a yawn,
as if it knew I was coming,
has seen me before,
can't be bothered to resist.

The forest parts like a curtain,
once drawn tight against the night,
now opening for the performance,
an invitation to applause.

The forest lies like a carpet,
like a bathmat, like a woman
used to being beaten, like a girl
who runs away from home.

The forest opens
and every tree holds out its leafy arms.

Stopping to Consider

Whose woods these are I think I know,
a line I learned at school
but never really considered.

Miles to go before.
Miles to go after.

Though I think I know now
there are no happy evers.
Only happy moments.

Bird song.
A spotted fawn
as dappled as the shade.
The oratorios of frogs.
A single butterfly.

And the deep thrumming
of the forest that too many people
mistake for silence.

Call and Response

I hear birds calling back and forth,
a *duet* I will later learn.
This is a place of correspondence,
perpetual conversation,
letters written in the air.

River asks a question,
rock asks one back.
Aspen asks birch, birch asks
bracken, bracken asks earth,
earth holds all the answers
tight against her breast.

I have questions I don't know
how to ask. There are answers
I don't know how to hear.
Here everything talks
at the same time.

I need to learn how to frame a question.
I need to learn how to listen.

Stones Across a Stream

The water sings as it rushes by.
If you drink me, you will become
a wolf, a fox, a deer.
Hunger brings strange dreams,
stranger longings.

Papa says water over twenty-one stones
becomes pure. People take longer.
Counting the stones, I step across.
There are only nineteen here.

Papa says we must become water.
I think I must become stone.

I want to get through Autumn
without having another fall from grace.

Here Where the Path of Healing Starts

This is the path of healing,
silver in the moonlight,
white stones glowing
like will-o-wisp
signposting the way.

On either side, pulses
of bloody trillium
warn the weary:
do not step out here,
do not stop out here.

Trees bend over with burdens
of old leaves, new,
baring shadow teeth,
whispering secrets
only trees can decode.

Behind, lies only
the cutting knife
devil's bargain,
severed past.

Behind, the clean words sulk
in their dishes of soap.
Bubbles burst on their way
to a stainless heaven.

Here the colors run riot,
little birds mob a hawk,
bats jitter on parade.
The forest is anything but silent.

I step onto the path,
knowing it is but the beginning,
one foot, then the other,
till I gleam silver all over,
in the moonlight,

starting with my hands.

Evening Meadow

The hallelujah chorus of birds,
a feathered symphony,
mossy grass beneath my feet,
trees standing silent watch
from the edges of the meadow.

A fox makes a parenthesis in the air,
hunting a meal. A woodpecker
jackhammers his invitation.
Leaves tremble when I pass
as if fearing contagion.

I am becoming a poet.
I am thinking in metaphors.
I am walking through a poem.

Learning the Words

The longer I am in these woods,
I learn words.
I become cornucopic
with language
which rolls around my mouth
like dark chocolate,
like butterscotch
like peppermint.

There's no one to caution my tongue,
no one to soap my mouth,
no one to bridle my brain.

Here I find such words as *smut,*
putrefaction, ordure, sludge,
all synonyms for filth
my father doesn't know.

But beautiful words, too:
allure, taradiddle, calliope,
mellifluous, dulcet, paradigm
which he has never spoken.

There is no end to such learning,
And no seeming end to these woods.

Little House in the Wood

It's unassuming, uninviting,
a pimple on the backside of the birch forest.
It makes no good first impression,
no impression at all. Reminds me
of a girl like me, on the first day of school,
on the last.

A light in a window, flickering,
smoke making curlicues above the chimney
like a child's first drawing of a house.
The little hut is fenceless, defenceless.
I am not afraid.

One step, two,
and then the house itself moves,
turning counter-clockwise,
widdershins,
shows me its door.
The lock grins open, baring its teeth.

It spits out a word.

CHAPTER FOUR

Meeting
the
Baba

That First Word

That first word hangs in the air
between the house and me,
droplets of spittle suspended
in the dusk.

Later, I learn *spittal* meant hospice,
hospital, journey's end,
so foreign I don't know
if it's clean or dirty,
whether welcome or warning.
I smile, say the magic word *Please,*
that all wheedling children know.

An upstairs light trembles.
Curtains twitch like eyelids reading text.
The door sticks out its tongue
testing for, tasting for honey,
then sighs with happiness,
lets me come in.

Knock Knock, Who's There

It's a joke, you know.
You don't know?
Knock knock,
Who's there?
Witch.
Witch who?
Not who.
Where's who?
Who's on second,
Which is on first.
Something like that.
I saw it on tv.
One of the few shows Papa allowed.
Two old guys,
one fat, one thin.
A routine, Papa called it.
Rhymes with clean.
Well, it was funny at the time.
Before the door was closed.
Was opened.

I See the Bony Hand First

I see the bony hand first,
knuckles broken on the wall of time.
Dirt under long fingernails.
It signals me in.

I see the crusted eyelids next,
the crafty blue eyes, so startling
in that face, wrinkled as the sea.
Hair the grey of winter waves.

And then she smiles.
It proves no improvement.
Cheekily, I smile back.
If she's surprised,
She doesn't show it, grunting
an animal acknowledgment.

It's invitation enough for me.

Meeting Baba Yaga

She's oceanic, a mighty force.
Teeth so full of fillings,
they might as well be made of iron.

Swollen knuckles on her fingers,
plain and round as worn wedding rings.
It aches to look at them.

She shuffles about in tired slippers
that slap at her heels like velvet-pawed cats.
Veins in her ankles broad as the River Don.

Eyes as light blue as a waterfall,
shot through with mica glints.
I cannot read her intent.

First she smells like a musty closet,
then like a garden of herbs,
tansy and thyme and the musk of sage.

I hold out my hand in greeting.
She grips it so hard, I wince,
whisper—*Damn!*

Papa's voice in my ear
saying, *Don't swear.*
I taste soap.

The old lady laughs.
You'll do, girl, you'll do.
And I do.

Touring the Little House

It's so much bigger than its seams,
room after room, appearing
along the hallway; river pearls
on a watery strand.

Here rooms grow like gourds
in a garden, all sizes, all shapes,
all colors, with windows in each wall,
no two ever the same.

It's so much bigger than it seems,
as if expansion, like a land war in Asia,
is the point of living here.
It seems I have a bed, bathtub, closet.

It seems she knew I was coming.
It seems the house knew how to prepare.
The Baba is unsurprised by seemings.
They are part of her witchy trade.

Chores

The Baba doesn't ask, just tells me,
the list as long as a death sentence,
but not as final.

Sweeping of course. And dusting.
A house that can walk about has rooms
full of sand, weeds, seedlings, burrs.

Making turnip soup each morning.
That ugly, prolific old root gives gladly,
like a missionary in a cannibal's clay pot.

Sprinkling poppy seeds around the foundation.
For the hut's protection, she says.
Get an alarm, I think, but don't say it out loud.

Washing the dishes, drying them on the cutting board.
For one old person, she uses a lot
of utensils, especially sharp knives.

Answering questions when the Baba asks.
After a while, I just make things up.
She seems to find that amusing.

Feisty Girls

Baba Yaga prefers them bright, asking questions,
challenging her, turning their backs.
She likes the ones who stick out their tongues,
laugh at death threats, use foul language, never beg.

She wants them to sweep the hut without whining,
empty the compost without complaint,
cook the soup, put a hand on the pestle,
learn to steer.

If they can sing the Volga Boatmen song,
dance the Kazachok without falling over,
recite Pushkin from memory,
know all the patronymics for Rasputin,
that's a plus.

Boys, on the other hand, she devours whole,
spitting out the little finger bones.
Even if they can dance and sing.
Even then.

The Baba's Iron Nose, Iron Teeth

Hey, old lady, that nose, those teeth
are pitted with age.
When did you last see a dentist?
You can't go out looking like that;
you'll scare the neighbors.

All I need is a strong polish,
some good grade wire wool,
soft brush, dishcloth, cotton gloves,
and a big tin of WD40.

All you have to do is lie back,
close your eyes, open wide,
think of the tsarina.

Trust me.
I'll do the rest.

Mortar/Pestle

Baba Yaga has never learned to drive a car
though she travels many miles each day,
sailing in her granite mortar, steered by a pestle.
The thing smells of crushed garlic, borscht,
dark Turkish cigarettes, kvass,
a Russian stew of bad habits, and tall tales.

No one sees her of course. She doesn't exist
unless you count bad dreams. Yet still she flies,
the friendly and unfriendly skies,
across tundra, taiga, major highways,
avoiding traffic jams, roundabouts,
only bothering the occasional helicopter
or low-flying private planes.

Now and then, aliens are reported,
or the government says she's a weather balloon,
or sometimes an incoming storm.
But that blip of unknown origin means
she's off to the grocery store or bingo parlor,
mahjong game, or bowling alley again.
Or maybe the latest superhero movie
though she says their teeth are too white, too even,
wonders how they can eat with those dainty choppers,
gnashes her own.

When she gets going nothing,
nothing stands in her way.

CHAPTER FIVE

Vasilisa

A Small Knock

The knock is small, barely a scratch,
I open the door without using the peephole.
On the doorstep, tentative, another girl.

I smile, usher her in. *Usher,* like a servant,
or the person at a play with a flashlight,
the one who shows you to your seat.

She smiles back and comes in, turns left,
always left, *widdershins* the Baba says,
walks the long hallway, finds a room.

It's as if she's been here before, knows her way,
or if she has dreamed of coming here,
who is, herself, as gossamer as a dream.

The room she turns in to is my room, now hers,
Like an explorer planting a flag. *We share,* she says.
Sisters. Companions. Cousins. Friends.

There is no word for what we are.

Saying Hello to the Other Girl

Hi.
Hi.
I've run.
I've come.
This house.
This hut.
My father.
You slut.
I hurt.
You hope.
I hate.
You dope.
I cut.
You ran.
From Father.
From man.
You know.
It's true.
We both.
We two.

Who knew?

In Vasilisa's Bed

So now there are two of us here, sharing a bed,
which grows larger the longer we lie in it.

Vasilisa, she says suddenly, singsong.
pointing to her tidy, perfect chest.
Natasha, I tell her. *The kids called me Nasty.*
Tash, she says. Never calls me anything else.

She's small and fine-boned as a china doll,
hair like flax, two fat braids, eyes grass and gold.
Not at all like me who grew large and lumpen,
dark from the firing of the kiln.

We are taken for sisters nonetheless.

How We Are Different, How the Same

I chew with my mouth open,
She chews with her mouth closed.
I snore in my sleep, or so she tells me.
She makes little mewing sounds, like a cat.
I like to walk outside, sit on a stone,
watch the river, make my mind go still.
She sings all day long, like a demented cuckoo,
like a Disney princess on crack.

She's magnet,
I'm iron.
We draw ever closer.
It's an uncomfortable,
comforting thought.

Being Sisters, Becoming Friends

We talk the first day. Tell jokes the second.
By the third we are truly sisters,
sharing my story, her story, history.
Turning our backs to one another
when we get undressed, dressed.

She gets the bigger part of the closet,
the major part of the bed, the first draw
of water in the shower, as if they are all her due.
Perhaps they are. I don't care.
It is the first time I have a sister.
A best friend.
Any friend.

Vasilisa's Doll

I came with nothing,
but bad memories
and an empty backpack.
Vasilisa's mother
gave her three things.
She never travels without them:
a tiny wooden doll,
last of a nesting trio;
an iron comb with teeth like hooks;
a blue ribbon the color of water.
Each came with a warning
which Vasilisa never shares.

Sometimes when she's asleep,
I run my fingers over the doll's head,
touch the iron tines, thread the ribbon
through my fingers.

But I never do this when she's awake
in case she'd mind.

The Mirror Knows Her Name

The mirror knows her name,
She's the Beautiful,
It tells her daily, but she doesn't answer.

She's like a princess
in an old Russian storybook
not pink tulle but embroidered robe.

She's the mystery jewel,
in the simple setting;
out of place, out of time,

out of my league.

An Oddness Between

There is something odd between them
The iron-nosed witch and the new girl.
Something angry, dark, secret.

A story I can't read.

I worry about ovens, about finger bones,
About what might be served in a stew.
But it is only the anger that simmers.

No one says a bad word at first.

Vasilisa laughs my fears away.
She's an old woman, afraid of the young,
she says, rolling the doll between her fingers.

Maybe it only seems odd.

She is cranky with age, Vasilisa says,
running the comb though the gold
of her jewel-like hair.

Beautiful, the mirror whispers.

The Baba just looks in the mirror,
finding only ugliness. The meanness
suddenly reminds me of high school gossip.

Nasty.

It rubs against me like a sore. I feel scabby,
but not enough to run, to shut another door,
not enough to leave my new, my only friend.

CHAPTER SIX

Settling In

This House Turns

This house turns whenever the Baba commands it,
spinning not so much like a top but a lazy Susan,
on a simple axis, spilling nothing.

She sits at the table, writing her lovelorn column,
never noticing the spin. Ink settles into the curves
of her letters, not a bit wasted.

Even walking across the floor, she's so practiced,
she doesn't miss her footing. We girls wonder at it,
as we slip, slide across the polished wood.

If there were a rug, we think, a big Persian,
even if it has to be tacked down,
it would help us finish our chores without a fall.

The old witch would never spend the money, though.
She's tight with her purchases, raises vegetables
in the big garden, and the meat—as we know too well—

comes knocking weekly at the front door.

Teaching Us to Drive

We crowd into the mortar which stretches itself
like a snake's mouth, a uterus, a birth canal,
to accommodate the three of us.

The Baba shows us the black iron starter,
the five gears, how the pestle steers.
how to stop without bumping into bushes.

Vasilisa, who says she's older than me,
gets to try driving first. She's good
at going forward, awful at parking.

I love the speed, can corkscrew through the trees,
make even Baba Yaga gasp at the loop-de-loops.
Tomorrow I plan to try wing-walking,

if only I can find some wings.

Cauldron

Baba Yaga doesn't use a cauldron,
though her grandmother did.
Stuck in her ways, the Baba calls her.

The Baba doesn't cook over flames,
So old-fashioned, she tells us,
preferring a reliable microwave.

She's got modern taps, and town water.
Who wants to carry buckets from a well?
she says from her sitz-bath.

She's remodeled the kitchen till it gleams
with chrome and stainless steel,
drawers that close by themselves.

At first it all seems like magic to us,
till she shows us the catalogs,
teaches us to read the fine print.

Baba Yaga's Garden

She grows rows of belladonna, liking the purple
flower bells, raised rainbow beds of foxglove,
monkshood.

Breathing deep of sawdust and smoke from
her beach apple tree, she makes autumn pies,
sets them on the window to cool.

Feeding her pitcher plants, she watches them
yawn open, smiles as they snap up her meaty
offerings.

Every day, she waters, prunes, deadheads,
weeds, digs in the compost, adds ground bone,
making her garden grow.

The sign on the Baba's garden gate says,
Come In. There is no sign that says
Exit.

Picking the Garden

My fingers have burns
from brushing past the smoking flamewort.
Vasilisa watches from the porch rocker,
crocheting a vest for Baba Yaga, laughing
as yet another thorn embeds itself
under one of my nails.

I cannot be angry with her
for taking the softer jobs.
My fingers tangle in yarn.
I fumble with needles,
cannot see the pattern
until it is done and laid flat.

Besides, I love the smell of fern
with its violin curl, the musk
of dusky roses before night
closes them down, don't mind
the scorch and scar of the garden
which I wear like medals of war.

Her Cousin's House of Candy

Baba Yaga's cousin has a house made out of candy.
Very uncomfortable, the Baba says. The walls sag
in wet weather and the cousin has to re-ice it every fall.
The birds continually peck out the door handles.
The keys never fit.

In the spring bears come by every morning
looking for a handout. *Or possibly a hand,* she mumbles.
The bone-yard fence is just asking for a call
from the building inspectors. They have cited her
half a dozen times already this year.

I never visit, the Baba tells us.
You would not believe
how dirty her ovens are.
She always eats the help.

Firebird in the Monkey Puzzle Tree

The droop of its red tail
almost sets the needles on fire.
Sparks burn the long fingers of the tree.
The roots shrink from the very idea
of a blaze.

The Baba can smell the singe
from her house. She fears that peasants
have found where she lives,
runs out the front door,
waving a stick.

Shouts—*Get off my lawn,*
though it is a meadow in a forest,
not a lawn,
not even hers.

Baba Yaga Has Tea with Kostchai the Deathless

When Kostchai comes to call he brings roses,
mostly wilted by his breath which smells
like a mortuary. His eyes are still
as gravestones and as hard.

He calls her Baba Yaga, no nicknames,
gives a little half bow, dusts the chair
with his white handkerchief before sitting,
compliments her on the shine of the floor.

They sit across from one another,
glasses full of tea laced with plenty of sugar
and arsenic, talking about their latest operations.
Organ recitals, she calls it.

He complains the weather has been too hot,
she says nobody uses proper grammar any more,
he says the price of tea is outrageous.
She says someone tried to steal her pestle.

Vasilisa and I stay in the pantry like servants,
collect the dirty dishes, the glasses.
Later we launder the table cloth, mop the floor.
Vasilisa pockets the coins he sets on the sideboard.

They are gold, with the head of the tsar
looking to the left, where danger comes from.
When he goes, Kostchai kisses the Baba on the cheek.

It leaves a scar.

Chicken Feet

I think today I would like a seaside view,
the wind in my hair, Vasilisa and me
sitting on the front porch watching gulls
and the red sails of the Fifies drifting by.

How long do you suppose it will take
for the cottage to get there on its chicken feet?
I argue for horses' hooves, Arabian for fleetness,
or Clydesdales better suited for carrying
an entire house on its shoulders.
But will the iron-nose lady listen to me?
She's tougher than Clinton or Thatcher ever were.

Tradition, she says through gritted teeth.
Tradition, I say, *will not get you an easy trip
south to Brighton or Edinburgh or Atlantic City.
Still, if you have the time, and money
is no object, or comes with no objection,
chicken feet will do, I suppose.*

She laughs, raps my knuckles, says: *You rick.*
Vasilisa says, *You mean rock.*
The Baba glares at her. *They mean the same.*

CHAPTER SEVEN

A Prince
Not Very
Charming

The Prince Comes to Call

He's the same as all princes,
cheekbones like knives
that cut to the heart.
A way of talking that sounds as if
plums have taken root in his mouth.
His clothes have no wrinkles,
his hair curls like snails
around the shells of his ears.
He looks in every mirror he passes,
gives himself a wink.
His fingernails are pink,
with cuticles like smiley faces.
Dirt never sticks to his trousers.
He doesn't bruise.

Making Jokes

I say something funny about the prince,
then the Baba and I laugh.
When I say the same to Vasilisa,
her mouth goes suddenly sour,
like a lemon too long on the shelf.

I try another, and another,
thinking I have to find the right one.
Soon I can make lemonade
from her face. I fall silent.

He's a prince, she says,
as if it explains everything.
which of course it does.
Humor, it seems, does not change royalty,
does not supplant reality,
does not change the lusting heart.

I Consult the Baba

The prince and Vasilisa lock eyes.
Their fingers vine together.
They make small comforting noises
like a puddle of puppies
which makes Baba Yaga fart
in their general direction.

Surely not, I whisper to the Baba,
she isn't such a fool.

You do not understand the human heart,
she tells me. *It runs on lust
the way horses run on oats.
A necessary meal—but,
in the end, only grass.*

Vasilisa Argues with the Baba

"Every loving has a death sentence…"
—Ask Baba Yaga website

I'm hanging on your every utterance,
old lady with the iron teeth,
but this time you have gone too far.

All the other tales promise me that love
lasts beyond death, but your straight razor
has slit my throat and the truth bleeds out.

Death is an ending, not a beginning.
I'll try to remember this,
should I ever need to fall in love again.

The operative word is fall, I suppose.
No one your age who falls is expected to rise.

Baba Yaga Answers in Kind

Baba Yaga answers in kind, but without kindness,
something about age, something about gratitude,
something about honor, about how the world works.

She snorts and snarls, gnashes her iron teeth
until there are bright sparks and smoke in her mouth,
until her tongue burns with a vivid flame.

We back away from the conflagration.
I look for an extinguisher. Papa had one in every room.
Perhaps the little hut takes care of such things on its own.

Perhaps it is well used to dealing with the Baba's fire.

An Orchard Tryst

I see them in the orchard.
They've settled under
the Beach Apple
which makes him cough.

He hawks up phlegm
into a silken handkerchief
which he crushes into a ball
and throws away in the weeds.

Small white petals fall
all around them,
making a wedding canopy.
I watch them through the scrim.

Their shadows kiss,
tongues dodging in and out,
like little animals seeking
a comfortable shelter.

A thrush sings from a burning bush.
An old wolf lies down next to a lamb.
A peacock fans open his fancy tail.
Corny stuff like that.

When the prince gets down on one knee,
I turn away. There's no magic here.
What comes ever after will make
no one happy.

Especially me.

Silence in the House

There is silence in the house.
I recognize it, try to break it
with the worst words I know.
Even soap in the mouth
would be better than this.

Damn, I begin. *Shit.*
Double poop. Ass.
Baba Yaga looks at me
and laughs. Glances down
at her grimy fingernails
and slowly scratches one
against her iron nose.
The sound is worse
than the silence.
I wince.

Try these, she says.
Mudak, suka, dik.
She looks back and forth
between the prince
and Vasilisa, spitting
each word out as if
it tastes sour.
They don't notice,

both so engrossed
in looking at themselves
looking at themselves.

Yebat, she adds loudly.
The question is clear in my eyes.
She laughs. *I tell them get lost,*
she says, *or the equivalent.*
I guess in English, the word
begins with a percussive F.

And who, I think, can be silent now?

The Prince Is Too

The prince is too old to be eaten,
Too big to be beaten,
too powerful to be killed,
too strong to be carted away.

He's too wary to be caught,
too knowing to be fooled,
too well-armed to be pricked,
too deep in lust to leave.

He eats his own food,
carries his own drink in a thermos,
grinds his own coffee beans,
sleeps with his back against the wall.

He knows what he wants,
will get what he came for
whether it's one girl or two.

Princes always do.

Vasilisa Dreaming

In the big bed, sleeping beside me,
Vasilisa dreams. She makes kissing noises,
touches my shoulder with her small hand,
palm down. I can feel the heat through my gown.

She sighs, turns over, murmurs the prince's name,
Ivan, which doesn't sit prettily in her mouth,
being both egocentric and brutal.
It comes out covered in spit.

He'll leave her for someone younger, prettier,
but not today.

She'll leave him for someone older, richer,
already a king. But not tomorrow.

I feel her restlessness until I fall asleep.
When I wake, the bed is small, her side cold.
She's gone on that long road into adulthood
from which none of us returns.

CHAPTER EIGHT

The Runaways

Running Away From, Running Towards
In Eight Fits

1.
Get up, the Baba yells, her words
derricking me into morning.
I leap into my clothes, have no time
to lace my shoes, or drink a cup of wakeup,
before we're running out the door.

You drive, she says, by which I know
she wants speed. *I'll tell you where.*
The mortar is sluggish at first,
but soon we're careening along
the lanes of sky. Traffic's light.
I can see the wind.

2.
There, she says, words strained by air.
She points to the two riding below,
Vasilisa behind, holding him tight.
I lean on the pestle and like a hawk
we make a great, steep stoop,
dropping toward our prey.

I feel the mortar flex and stretch.
Readying for the pounce,
I bank slightly to the right

Then straighten like a teacher's ruler.
The prince looks up, but Vasilisa looks ahead.
The horse's sides are thick with sweat.

3.
Then Vasilisa, silly, cunning girl,
looks up, loosens her hold
on the prince for a single moment,
takes out her mother's comb.
She mumbles words I can't make out,
flings the comb behind.

A strange forest of Norway pine
grows swiftly, raising green fists,
making a leafy barrier, a portcullis of limbs.
We must thread our way through
if we're to keep them in sight.
The horse's sides are streaming foam.

4.
In every forest's beginning, is its end.
The horse emerges from the woods at last.
Down! Baba Yaga shouts,
pointing a finger bony as an arrow.
She is puffing like a chimney
from the gnashing of her iron teeth.

Again, I push the lever forward,
We bolt like lightning seeking its target,

like a bullet shot from a sniper's gun,
like a missile from a man-less drone.
like Thor's hammer loosed from his fist.
We become Death, destroyer of worlds.

5.
This time Vasilisa, that cunning girl,
throws the blue ribbon behind.
It falls into the ground, burrows under,
rises up again as a freshet, a spring,
a cascade, a waterfall, then a river
vaster, more twisty than the Volga.

It twines and vines about them.
Witches can't cross running water,
a rule I didn't know till the Baba curses,
her spittle falling like rain into the rill below
Widdershins, she cries, *always left.*
So I bank and take us the long route around.

6.
We see them again just as they reach the palace,
with its sweep of vast green lawns,
the spires of its towers jousting with the clouds.
I throw us down like a noble's glove
ready to slap the prince's face,
to force the necessary duel.

He looks up and raises a hand,

reaches for his bow, stands up in the stirrup,
shoots a faulty arrow that falls into the earth.
It doesn't bode well for children, I think, and laugh.
But the Baba sighs. She sees what I do not.
The horse's sides are flecked with blood.

7.
Then Vasilisa, that cunning girl,
casts behind her the little wooden doll
which becomes a hedgehog of spears,
a concatenation of cannons,
an army of automatons immune
to all of the Baba's magic.

We're both done and undone.
I haul the pestle backwards
with a heavy hand and hard heart.
Riding swiftly home, through darkened skies.
we fling ourselves into a future
without the other girl.

8.
The horse will be well stabled tonight,
the girl well bedded, the prince well pleased.
There may be a wedding or not, a baby or two.
A kingdom won or lost. It's no longer our concern
I may weep alone in my room, but the Baba
shouldn't care. She never liked the girl.
I don't know why.

CHAPTER NINE

Ever After

We Plot Revenge

On the table is bat guano
With it we can make bombs.
Amanita for poison.
Eye of toad for a spell.

I could find a gun, I say.
Get a carrying permit.
No one checks in this state.

We stare into the crystal,
see the death of dreams.
Even I can read that future.

After a day and a night of it,
the Baba writes in her column
Living well lasts longer than love.

I want to question her thesis,
but have no facts to support an argument.
I sit silent, chew on my thumb.

We store the guano in the byre,
amanita in the pantry,
talk no more of guns.

We bury the toad's eye in the garden

to ward off rabbits, deer.
Next we will try and live well enough.

Even if what the Baba says
isn't true,
we have to try.

A Bed for Weeping

The bed is cold without her,
sleep long, dreams dark.
I turn the nightlight on.

An echo of my tears
threads down the hall.
The Baba is a river in spate.

We don't speak of it in the morning,
carefully closing the floodgate door,
making certain the dike holds.

We climb into a little boat
that will carry us across this gray river,
each pulling on a separate oar.

Writing Poems, Telling Lies

1.
The Baba gives me paper,
and a pen that sputters ink.

Write, she says, *tell the true*
Though you may have to lie to do it.

I make a blobby start, doing as she says.
How hard can it be?

As it turns out, very hard.
Hardest of all is to begin.

2.
I think of Papa and start to write:
Come to the altar of the book,
open your heart, take in the story
It's a transubstantiation
as great as any you believe in.

How can this be, this great magic,
that makes real the unreal, the not-actual
into a kind of factless fictual,
turns lies into the True?

Don't ask me, for I am new at this work,
new at telling my own truth.

All I can start with is Once Upon A Time,
that oldest and truest of lies.

3.
I think of Mama and write some more:

Like the piano player, I have memory
in my fingertips. I watch words spill out
creating worlds, inventing colors,
bridging generations.

I write *tree,* and it grows
from seed to bole to fruit
in a moment, needing neither spring
nor sunshine to sprout.

I write *battle* and armies—
armed and armored—spring up
before a single piece of metal
can be forged.

Once I wrote a seventeen page novel
in seventh grade, stitching together
all the books I'd ever loved.
You didn't save it, Mama,

but the memory of creation is here
in my fingers, as they hold fast
to the feather weight
of Baba Yaga's pen.

Finally, I Ask Baba Yaga

I've many questions, but am not eager
to know the Baba's answers.
They'll be hard kernels between my teeth.
Biting down becomes a question of physics,
a reply only dentists can give.

I feel a query under my tongue,
rough-edged, slightly salty,
like a loosened tooth.
Vasilisa, I wish it were your tongue.

Perhaps that is the answer I'm seeking.
The only answer.

Baba Yaga Tells the Future

She looks into a glass of water,
floats a blood-red petal, pushes it
like a toy boat with her quill pen.

She scrys through a water glass
as if reading the book of life, afterlife,
as if the future is crystal, is clear.

She runs her forefinger with its iron nail
across my palm till it raises a welt,
then licks the welt to make the blood come.

She yanks out three of her teeth,
casts them on the table like dice, laughing
when they come up craps.

Takes the Farmer's Almanac off the shelf,
riffles through its pages.
The weather informs her prognostications.

Last, she shuffles her tarot deck,
finds the hanged man, turns the card around,
holds him to the light.

Says: *Telling the future is dead easy, girl,
easier when you're already dead inside.*

Finally, I Think About Baba Yaga's Tears

They were not like human tears,
more like blood, like fire,
bright red and smoking,
running down her cheeks and leaving scars.

You did not even want her here, I say.
And yet she was feisty, stood up to you.

She smiles ruefully at me. Ruefully.
It's not a word I've ever used before.
It sits between us like an unwanted guest
at the dinner table.

She's my daughter, the Baba says.

That should have surprised me, but it doesn't.
Instead it is the final piece of the puzzle,
the one that looks as if it can't possibly fit,
yet when you rotate it, suddenly it does.

Will she come back? I whisper.
Bad pennies always do, she tells me.
Then, finger against her nose, adds:
She'll break your heart all over again.

But not tomorrow, I say, knowing that to be true.
The Baba smiles, nods, but doesn't laugh.
Not when you want her, but when you don't.

Going Widdershins

I sit down and scribe a letter,
with scratches and blots,
and a certain amount of love
telling Mama I'm safe, warm.

I sign it, *With lots of love*
but no longer yours, Tash
Post it early morning
when Papa is deep in dreaming,
dropping the letter and my key
onto the doorstep of the house
as the mortar hovers above.

I circle three times going widdershins,
just because I want to,
just because I can.
I do it well.

I've finally learned to forgive.
I haven't yet learned to spell.

Baba Yaga Swears

Baba Yaga swears at objects:
a rug that dares to trip her,
a branch that reaches out trembling fingers
to slap her across the face.
She curses stones that shake
as she crosses the river,
lights that dare shine in her eyes,
a sour piece of fruit, thorn beneath the nail,
a knife that cuts too close to the bone.

She doesn't swear at people.
That's what spells are for, she says
as she teaches me the words.

Turn to Me

I have learned to lean into the hut's turnings.
The first time I was dizzy with it,
It felt like the moment the boy you crush on
walks towards you in the high school hall,
never noticing your befuddles.
Or the girl you think of as yours dazzles
with a perfect ten point smile.

The second time I felt a slight rise, as in a fever.
The third, a small knock at the door.
Now it is like living on a house boat:
the swell of waves, the turn of tides,
a moment of emotion, with the "e" removed.

Tomorrow the Baba promises she will teach me
the words of summoning, so I can make
the little house turn to me on command.

Not shazam, not abracadabra,
but something simple to remember,
yet dead easy to forget.

Finding the Inner Witch

Now we read to one another, finishing Pushkin,
going on to Dostoyevsky. Afterwards we try Gaiman,
Austen, Rowling, Pullman, even Stephen King.
She teaches me how to parse a sentence,
how to identify a gerund, how to cut back on adverbs,
how to write columns, how to parse poems,
how to spell.

I've learned to write poetry, telling the truth
through metaphor, simile, straight-forward lies.

We play cards, work in the garden.
I make more raised beds, liking the feel
of wood beneath my fingers, the sawdust smell.
She shows me the way to plant the herbs.
I take up knitting, make her a shawl.
It is full of knots. She says she likes it that way.
She sings to the balalaika in a reedy tenor voice,
songs of longing for the motherland.
I learn to embroider, I learn to scry.
I'm woeful at both, but she doesn't tell me so.

We are like an old couple now, an odd couple,
the oddest. Are we sisters? Cousins?
Mother and child? It doesn't matter,

for I crossed tundra, taiga, major highways,
nineteen stones and a meadow
to find this home.

She promises me I'll be the Baba ever after.
For now that's quite enough.

Coda

You Think You Know This Story

So, *this* is a tale
both old and new,
borrowed, narrowed,
broadened, deepened,
rethreaded, rewoven,
stitches uneven,
re-plastered, re-harled,
rehearsed, reworked
until it's my own.

Love comes through a back door,
leaves by the front.
Not all baptisms occur at the font.
Witches are made, of blood and bone.
Witches are made, not only born.
A story is, not always means.
We pass on our genius
as well as our genes.

You think you know this story.
You hope you know this story.
You want to tell this story,
perhaps now you will.

Reading Group Guide

A Tor.com Book/Published by Tom Doherty Associates
Reading Guide for *Finding Baba Yaga* by Jane Yolen
Grades 9–12

ABOUT THIS GUIDE

The questions and activities that follow are intended to enhance your reading of *Finding Baba Yaga,* a novella in verse by Jane Yolen. This guide has been developed in alignment with the Common Core State Standards; however please feel free to adapt this content to suit the needs and interests of your students.

SYNOPSIS

In *Finding Baba Yaga,* the stories of modern runaway Natasha and Russian fairy tale witch Baba Yaga intersect in a poetic journey. Reminiscent of the artful design of a Russian matryoshka nesting doll, elements of Slavic myth, Russian folklore, and fairy tales cleverly fit into the contours of a contemporary narrative in Jane Yolen's verse novella. Powerful individual poems scaffold into a rich story that explores the sometimes fragile, fraught bonds of parents and children, motherhood, and sisterhood; the bittersweet transition from child to adult; the nature and power of religion, language, and story; and the ambiguous identity and morality of Baba Yaga herself. The literary genres and poetic styles in this unique novella twist and turn much like Baba Yaga's ambulatory, chicken-footed hut. It's as if *Finding Baba Yaga*'s dynamic ingredients, from existential to everyday, from the magical to the mundane, and from mythic to modern, have been ground together by Baba Yaga's mortar and pestle itself. You think you're in narrator Natasha's contemporary reality, when author Jane Yolen "turns the fables" on you, and sends Natasha on a trail—or is it through a tale—to learn to write (or, *Finding Baba Yaga* invites you to consider, perhaps to "right") her own story.

PREREADING DISCUSSION QUESTIONS

1. *Finding Baba Yaga* is a novella in verse. Have you read other verse books? How was that reading experience similar to reading "standard" prose fiction? How was it different? Do you prefer one to the other? If so, why?

2. Baba Yaga is one of the most famous, and infamous, characters in Russian folklore. Her roots can be traced to Slavic myths and pre-Christian pagan traditions. Modern culture has also appropriated this ancient persona, who can be a force of good or evil; a source of guidance or grief; a witch or godmother, albeit one who is more "scary" than "fairy." Baba Yaga, or variations of her image and character, appear in movies, comics, and merchandise. Have you encountered Baba Yaga in any of these literary or commercial contexts? What are your impressions of this perennial witch character?

3. If you haven't encountered Baba Yaga, is there a fairy tale story or character that has stayed with you since early childhood? Which character or tale? Why do you think fairy tale characters, stories, or symbols can have such "staying power" in personal and cultural memory and imagination?

POSTREADING DISCUSSION QUESTIONS

1. Why do you think author Jane Yolen chose to write *Finding Baba Yaga* in verse form?

2. From your reading of the first poem, "You Think You Know This Story," do you think the author would argue that more

gets lost, or found, in translation of stories from oral to written; between cultures; through time; when they scale from personal to universal, or vice versa? Why do you think this poetic "prologue" emphatically distances *Finding Baba Yaga* from fairy tale tropes like charming princes and magic wands?

3. In Chapter One, what does the poem "Soap in the Mouth" reveal about the relationship between the narrator (Natasha) and her father? How does "The Taste That Lingers" explore the power of language? How does the next poem, "Behind a Closed Door," discuss language's *lack* of power? In "Fence of Bones," Natasha envisions her mother aging into a wizened, cronelike condition, and Natasha calls her a "witch." Why do you think Ms. Yolen chooses to evoke these vivid parallels between Natasha's mother and Baba Yaga?

4. In Chapter Two, the poem "This Is Not a Fairy Tale" revisits the opening poem's rejection of fairy tale stereotypes. In light of this persistent metacognition on whether or not *Finding Baba Yaga* is, itself, a fairy tale, how do you interpret the last line of Chapter Two's final poem, "The Last Road": "Like the hero in any good tale, I boldly walk in"?

5. The poems in Chapter One and Chapter Two root the narrative in a modern moment and realistic setting, with attention to gritty details about a family in distress, and a runaway's physical and emotional dislocation. Why do you think the author organizes the poems in Chapter Three under the title "Into the Woods," which recalls fairy tale "poster child" Red Riding Hood's path to her grandmother's house?

6. In Chapter Three's "Evening Meadow," the narrator reflects: "I am becoming a poet. I am thinking in metaphors. I am walking through a poem." Do you think this observation foreshadows the narrator's, or the narrative's, transition from "real

life" to (borrowing a term Ms. Yolen uses in the foreword) "storyland"? What does it suggest to you about how story relates to reality, or the concept of a person's "life story"?

7. In Chapter Four, Natasha arrives at Baba Yaga's "mobile" home. Traditionally, Baba Yaga asks visitors to her hut on chicken legs if they have come to her accidentally or intentionally. Do you think fate or free will brings Natasha to Baba Yaga? Why?

8. Who do you think Vasilisa (who enters the story in Chapter Five) is to Natasha, literally or symbolically? Why do you think the narrator's name is revealed so late in the story (in the Chapter Five poem "In Vasilisa's Bed"), even though Natasha is arguably the protagonist of the piece, rather than the eponymous Baba Yaga?

9. Why do you think Jane Yolen puts four poems in a row (starting with "Her Cousin's House of Candy") in Chapter Six that are all distinctly fairy tale fare? Would you argue that Natasha is in a fairy tale or a nightmare?

10. How does Prince Ivan's arrival in Chapter Seven alter the dynamics of the odd little trio Baba Yaga, Natasha, and Vasilisa had "settled into" in Chapter Six?

11. Why do you think the author titles Chapter Eight "The Runaways," echoing Chapter Two's title, "The Runaway"? What do you infer from the notable omission of "Happily" in Chapter Nine's title, "Ever After"?

12. How do you interpret the Chapter Nine poem, "Finding the Inner Witch"? Is Natasha's search really for Baba Yaga, or is it perhaps a journey to find her *own* inner voice, strength, and truth? Do you think the coda, "You Think You Know This Story," is an invitation to the reader to write their own story—perhaps the *only* story anyone can truly know?

COMMON CORE–ALIGNED READING
LITERATURE, WRITING & RESEARCH ACTIVITIES

These Common Core–aligned activities may be used in conjunction with the pre- and postreading questions above.

I: SLAVIC MYTH AND RUSSIAN FOLKLORE

A. *Finding Baba Yaga*'s Roots in Eastern Europe

1. Have students do a research project to explore a self-generated question or thesis based on one of the suggested subjects, or a related topic. Organize data from online and library research into a multimedia presentation for the class. Or, have students write a research paper reporting, and reflecting on, their findings.

    Suggested subjects: the relationship between Slavic Myth and Russian Folklore; transition/tension between Russian paganism and Christian orthodoxy; how this cultural legacy is manifest in characters, themes, or symbolism in *Finding Baba Yaga*; the path from oral storytelling traditions to written fairy tales in Eastern European cultural history; Vladimir Propp's *Morphology of the Fairy Tale*, and how *Finding Baba Yaga* conforms to, or diverges from, key conventions outlined; Linda J. Ivanits's "double faith" thesis, and how it might relate to some of the tensions, particularly with respect to religion, language, and nature, explored in *Finding Baba Yaga*'s poetic commentary; compare/contrast Alexander Afanasyev's *Russian Fairy Tales* with the Western European fairy tale collections of the Brothers Grimm.

2. Revisit the text of *Finding Baba Yaga* to select a literary or cultural reference, symbol, character, or term that has Slavic or Russian roots (byliny, burlak, kazachok, Volga River, Skakza, tsar, or tsarina, for example). Write a brief essay to define it,

discuss its historical, cultural, and/or literary significance, and explain its role and relevance in *Finding Baba Yaga*.

3. Through online and library research, find a Russian tale featuring a character that appears in *Finding Baba Yaga* (such as Baba Yaga, Vasilisa, Kostchai the Deathless, Firebird, Ivan). In a 2–3 page essay, compare and contrast the treatment of the character in the traditional Russian tale with their modern reimagining in Jane Yolen's *Finding Baba Yaga*. Cite specific details and examples, from *both* texts, as you analyze your chosen character's role in plot and theme; relationship to protagonist; characterization as good or evil; attitude, attributes, and appearance. If desired, use your background research to develop a multimedia "Character Sketch" to help classmates gain a richer understanding of the character's role beyond the two texts, in the larger cultural landscape. Remember to include their literary origins, counterparts in other cultures, and modern analogues if applicable.

B. Revisiting Baba Yaga: Matriarch, Mentor, or Monster? Witch, Is It?

1. In the foreword, author Jane Yolen shares that her inspiration for *Finding Baba Yaga* was the website http://fairytalenews blog.blogspot.co.uk, "which features an ongoing set of weekly posts voiced by Baba Yaga as a Lonely Hearts columnist. Originally posted on The Hairpin, "Ask Baba Yaga" has since been collected and published as *Ask Baba Yaga: Otherworldly Advice for Everyday Troubles* by Taisia Kitaiskaia (Andrews McMeel, 2017). Keeping this in mind, ask students to write a short essay, citing relevant lines, verses, and textual evidence, describing how Baba Yaga inhabits that lonely-hearts-writer role in Ms. Yolen's *Finding Baba Yaga*.

2. Invite students to write a narrative in which they put Baba Yaga in another contemporary role, such as taxi driver, lawyer, guidance counselor, or some such. What protagonist comes to her? What kind of advice or direction are they seeking, and does this "version" of Baba Yaga help or hinder them?

3. Jane Yolen has written other books in which Baba Yaga is featured: the children's picture book *The Flying Witch*, the graphic novel *Curses Foiled Again*, and the adult novel (written with Midori Snyder) *Except the Queen*. Invite students to see if they can find one of these books and talk about how Baba Yaga, that protean folktale character, plays many different roles.

II: POETIC FORMS AND LITERARY DEVICES

A. *Inspiration, Variation, and Combination*

1. Develop a chart that outlines definitions and key features of poetic forms such as: prose, narrative, or lyrical poems; free verse; sonnets; odes; ballads; and epics. Using the chart as a reference, write a short essay analyzing how specific poems, or sections, from *Finding Baba Yaga* echo or embody elements of one or more of these classic forms.

2. Ask students to write an essay analyzing how Jane Yolen deploys specific literary techniques or poetic devices in *Finding Baba Yaga*. In their essays, students can focus on one or several devices, such as alliteration, consonance, simile, wordplay, metaphor, irony, or allegory, for example. Or students might consider how Jane Yolen uses poetic "tools" like number of lines, length and number of stanzas, rhyme scheme, or subject matter. Discuss how she uses these to advance the plot, examine recurring themes, create aesthetic or

dramatic effect, or develop characters. Students can focus on one poem, or track the use of a technique throughout *Finding Baba Yaga,* being sure to cite explicit examples, as well as making inferences from their reading of the text.

B. Poetic Perspective

1. On her website (janeyolen.com), Jane Yolen includes these two tips for writing poetry:

   > "Look at the world through metaphor."
   > "Tell the truth inside out or on the slant."

   Ask students to write an essay that explains how, where, and why they think Jane Yolen used these strategies in *Finding Baba Yaga.* Remind them to reference specific lines, stanzas, poems, or chapters, which illustrate these tips in action.

2. Invite students to try their hand at writing a poem using one or both of these tips.

III GENRES, THEMES, AND SYMBOLISM

A. A Varied Tale

1. *Finding Baba Yaga* combines elements of American realism, magical realism, fairy tale, and fable. Ask students which genre they think plays the most dominant role in *Finding Baba Yaga.* Have them do online and library research on that genre, identify its key features, and write an essay explaining how *Finding Baba Yaga* fits into the category.

2. Identify a key theme or symbol from *Finding Baba Yaga* (such as, the nature and power of language and story; the journey

from childhood to adulthood; the relationship between religion and language; "good" and "bad" words; the unique dynamics of female friendships and mother/daughter relationships; the woods; stones and water; a recurring fairy tale image or reference). In an essay, explain why you think that theme or symbol is significant in *Finding Baba Yaga*; and cite specific lines, poems, or chapters that illustrate how it is introduced and developed in the text.

Supports Common Core State Standards: W.9-10.2, 9-10.2A, 9-10.3, 9-10.7, 9-10.9, 9-10.9A, 11-12.1; RL.9-10.1, 9.10.2, 9-10.3, 9-10.4, 9-10.7, 11-12.5; CCRA (College & Career Readiness Anchor Standard).R.5, CCRA.R.6.

About the Author

JASON STEMPLE

JANE YOLEN is a bestselling, beloved, and immensely prolific author of more than 365 books for children, teens, and adults, including the picture book *How Do Dinosaurs Say Goodnight?* and the novels *The Devil's Arithmetic* and *Briar Rose*. She is also a poet, a teacher of writing and literature, and a reviewer of children's literature. She has been called "the Hans Christian Andersen of America" (by *Newsweek*) and "the Aesop of the twentieth century" (by the *New York Times*). Six colleges and universities have given her honorary doctorates for her body of work. One of her awards set her good coat on fire. She blames Baba Yaga for that.

TOR · COM

Science fiction. Fantasy. The universe.

And related subjects.

*

More than just a publisher's website, *Tor.com*
is a venue for **original fiction, comics,** and
discussion of the entire field of SF and fantasy,
in all media and from all sources. Visit our site
today—and join the conversation yourself.